Mama Rex & T

 ## The Sort-Of Super Snowman

by Rachel Vail
illustrations by Steve Björkman

SCHOLASTIC INC.
New York Toronto London Auckland Sydney
Mexico City New Delhi Hong Kong Buenos Aires

To Dad, who has always understood about magic.
—*RV*

To Rachel, who has a heart for the child's heart.
—*SB*

ISBN 0-439-38472-9

10 9 8 7 6 5 4 3 2   02 03 04 05 06

Printed in the U.S.A.
First Scholastic edition, December 2002

Book design by Elizabeth Parisi

Contents

Chapter 1
GET OUT

Outside, everything was white.

Inside, nothing was. Mama Rex was deep within T's closet, digging for his snow pants.

"I know they're in here somewhere," yelled Mama Rex. "I put them in a safe place last spring, so I wouldn't have to go searching, and I'm fairly — aha!"

T turned away from the window. He had been watching the fat snowflakes falling.

Piles of stuffed animals and parts of toys and a few old socks fell off Mama Rex's back as she stood up and backed out of the closet, holding something.

Mama Rex and T looked at the thing. It looked like a tired, linty snake.

Mama Rex turned it the other way. She reached inside it and yanked.

Now it looked like two tired, linty snakes, kissing.

"My cozy blues!" yelled T, hugging them. "I've been looking for these sweats."

"Well, I found them," said Mama Rex. "Now if only I could find your snow pants, we could go enjoy the day."

Mama Rex dove back into the closet.

T flopped down on his bed, cuddling his cozy blues. He was already enjoying the day.

There was no school because of the snow, and no work for Mama Rex.

T picked up his flashlight and his new library book, *The Super Snowman*, and scrambled under his covers.

"Got 'em!" yelled Mama Rex. "T?"

T peeked out from under the covers.

"Maybe we could stay home," suggested T.

"It's a beautiful winter day," said Mama Rex.
"We could go skating, or sledding... have
a snowball fight... "

"Or," said T, "we could make hot
chocolate and watch a video."

Mama Rex looked at the snow pants in her hand.
The tags were still on.

"No way, T," said Mama Rex, yanking off the
tags. "This is what happened all last winter, too,
and I'm going to go stir-crazy if we sit in this
apartment all day. We are going out and having
fun today, whether you like it or not!"

Mama Rex handed the snow pants to T. "Anyway, we don't have any hot chocolate mix."

T looked up at her sadly.

"Come on, T. When I was your age, playing in the snow felt magical."

"Not to me," said T, wrapping his blanket around him. "To me it feels cold."

"I took out your long underwear," said Mama Rex. As she left T's room, she added, "We're out of here in five minutes."

"We could order in Chinese food," yelled T.

"Four and three-quarters," Mama Rex yelled back.

T started pulling on all the clothes that Mama Rex had laid out for him. The long underwear was soft, and so were the first socks.

Then T put on his cozy blues and the wool socks.

Then he put on the turtleneck, the sweater, the fleece, the vest, the snow pants, the jacket, the neck-warmer, and the hat.

T could see his boots beside his leg, but he
could barely move.

He stepped onto one boot, but his foot
wouldn't go in. He bent over to grab the top of
the other boot, tipped forward, and landed in a
heap on his floor.

Mama Rex ran in to see what the loud thump
had been. "Is there a dinosaur in all that?"
she asked.

"Murmph," T managed to say.

Mama Rex helped T up and shoved the boots onto his feet. "This is fun already," she said, wiggling mittens onto T's hands. "Right?"

"Um..." said T.

Mama Rex tripped over T's book on her way to the door. "What's this?"

"*The Super Snowman*," said T, pointing at the cover with his mittened hand.

"Hey!" said Mama Rex. She tucked the book under her arm and grabbed her pocketbook. "This gives me a great idea!"

"Uh-oh," said T, lumbering behind her down the hall, toward the elevator.

Chapter 2
THE SNOW

"Ooh!" said T, as he stepped into the snowy day.

"Ahh," said Mama Rex, right behind him.

Big, fat snowflakes fluttered down in no hurry at all.

T tipped his head back and caught one on his tongue. "Tasty," he commented.

"Let's make a Super Snowman," said Mama Rex. "Like in your book."

"It's not *Super* as in *terrific*," explained T. "It's *Super* as in *Superhero*. This snowman rescues people."

"Oh," said Mama Rex, opening the book.

T slapped his mitten on a page. "The Super Snowman is rescuing this girl who's lost on the beach. He has to be really fast because — see? He's melting."

"Wow," said Mama Rex. "What an unfortunate job for a snowman."

T laughed. "Yeah. Even more unfortunately, his favorite food is soup!"

Mama Rex sniffled. "Soup sounds good. It's pretty cold out, huh?"

"Not to me!" said T. "Should we have a snowball fight instead?"

"No," said Mama Rex. "Let's build our own version of a Super Snowman."

"We can't. We don't have any magic dust," said T, "to make him come alive."

"Oh, yeah?" Mama Rex whispered. "What do you think all that shmootz is at the bottom of my pocketbook?"

T's eyes opened wide. "Really?"

Mama Rex shrugged humbly. "I don't know. Maybe."

"We could try," said T.

T knelt down and gathered up a big clump of snow. "Let's roll it," T said. "We need a huge, round ball for the bottom."

Mama Rex piled the book and her pocketbook on a bench and crouched down to help T.

They rolled.
They patted.
They gathered more.
They sneezed.

They stood up to look.
"Hmmm," said Mama Rex.
"Bleh," said T. "It's a triangle."

Mama Rex clapped her hands together.

"It's terrible," said T. "Why are you applauding?"

"I'm not. My fingers are cold," explained Mama Rex. "Maybe we should do more clumping and less rolling."

"Yeah," agreed T. "That'd be much better."

So they clumped.

They clumped and clumped and clumped.

They stood back to look.

"Hmmm," said Mama Rex.

"Bleh," said T. "It's a snow lump."

T stamped his feet.

"Don't get frustrated," said Mama Rex.

"I'm not," said T. "My toes are cold."

"He just needs something," said Mama Rex, marching over to the bench. She opened the book and studied a picture of the Super Snowman.

T peeked around Mama Rex as she searched through her pocketbook. "What are you getting?" asked T.

"Aha!" said Mama Rex, and pulled out — four old animal crackers.

"Uh," said T, "I don't think..."

But Mama Rex paid no attention. She marched
over to the lump and stuck the animal crackers
in a row down his middle.

"Buttons?" asked T.

"Exactly," said Mama Rex, heading back to her
pocketbook.

"Now what?" asked T.

"Lipstick!" announced Mama Rex.

"No!" yelled T, following her. "He's a boy!"

"It's a neutral color," said Mama Rex, drawing
a mouth on him.

Then Mama Rex dug through her pocketbook some more.

She found a short old pencil stub, which she handed to T.

"To draw his nose?" asked T.

"Sure," said Mama Rex.

T tried to draw a nose on the snow lump. Nothing showed up.

He drew and drew, but managed only to scrape a little dent.

T stabbed the whole pencil in, until only the eraser showed. A small hunk of the Snowman's face fell off.

"That's OK," said Mama Rex. "He needed to lose a little weight."

T ran back to look with Mama Rex in her pocketbook. "What about the eyes?" he asked.

"I'm looking," said Mama Rex.

She found a used tissue, some coupons, a wallet, a date book, three electronic gadgets, two toy cars, one linty mint, sixty-three receipts, and a lot of schmootz.

"I'm sorry, T," said Mama Rex. "I guess we're out of luck." Shivering, Mama Rex sat down on the bench.

"Wait!" said T. "That gives me a great idea."

T pulled off his mittens, dropped them on the ground, dug into his pockets, and found a penny in each. "I keep them there to rub for good luck," he said.

"How lucky," said Mama Rex, and sneezed.

T ran over to the Snowman, reached up, and wedged the pennies in.

One slid down a bit. The other went in too deep.

T and Mama Rex stood back to look.

"Hmmm," said Mama Rex.

"Bleh," said T. "He's a mess."

Mama Rex and T stared at their lopsided, lumpy Snowman.

The snow had stopped falling, and they were cold and wet. But slowly a smile spread across T's face.

He looked up at Mama Rex and whispered, "The magic dust."

Chapter 3
THE MAGIC

Mama Rex shook her head. "T," she said. "I have to admit something."

But T wasn't listening. He was running back to the bench, to Mama Rex's pocketbook.

Mama Rex beat him there and grabbed her pocketbook. "There's no magic dust in here, T."

"Yes, there is! I saw it!" He jumped up, trying to grab her pocketbook.

Mama Rex lifted her pocketbook above her head. "But, T..."

"Come on!" T jumped higher. "Let's throw the magic dust on him and make him come alive!"

"T!" said Mama Rex. "Stop!"

T stopped jumping. Mama Rex sat down on the bench, and T sat beside her.

Mama Rex took a deep, sad breath. "Do you know what the schmootz really is, in the bottom of my pocketbook?"

T nodded. "Magic dust."

"No, T," said Mama Rex. "It's mushed-up animal crackers and mints and lint and Cheerios. That's all."

T smiled up at Mama Rex. "That's just what it's made of," said T. "Those are the *ingredients*. Maybe those are the ingredients of magic dust."

"T," argued Mama Rex. "It's not..."

"Have you ever seen a recipe for magic dust?" asked T.

Mama Rex shook her head.

"Then you don't *know* it's not magic dust," reasoned T.

Mama Rex could not argue with that logic.

She handed her pocketbook to T. He opened it and scraped out a handful of schmootz.

She followed T as he carefully stepped toward the Snowman.

"Ready?" asked T.

"I just... I don't want you to be disappointed if he doesn't come to life," said Mama Rex, touching T's shoulder.

T lowered his hand. "Mama Rex," said T. "Magic dust is *pretend*."

"Right," said Mama Rex.

"So you have to *pretend*," explained T. "Get it?" Mama Rex nodded a little.

"You OK now?" asked T. Mama Rex nodded some more, so T threw the magic dust.

It flew toward the Snowman in an arc.

It sprinkled lightly into the nooks and crannies of the Snowman's lumpy head. It cascaded down the Snowman's bumpy body.

Mama Rex and T watched.

Nothing was happening.

But then, suddenly —

Snow started falling again.

Mama Rex and T blinked their eyes and looked up into the white sky.

"Wow," said Mama Rex. "Am I imagining that?

"If you are, I'm imagining the same thing," said T. "Cool."

As the fat snowflakes swirled around them,
Mama Rex and T held hands. After a few
minutes, Mama Rex and T were both really cold.
"Want to go in?" asked Mama Rex. "Or should
we go out for some hot chocolate first?"
"I was thinking we could have pretend hot
chocolate at home," said T.

Mama Rex shrugged. "OK by me." She picked
up her pocketbook.

"But let's go out," said T. "Real stuff is fun
sometimes, too."

"Sure is," said Mama Rex.

So Mama Rex and T turned around and walked
through the falling snow, past their sort-of
super, definitely magic snowman, in search of
a warm café.